LITTLE CHIEF
and Ogopogo

Dedication:

Dedicated with love to my family, friends, and
students, including many internationally, who
have become family. I delight in you all.

—D. T.

Also by Delores Topliff:

Whoosh

Little Big Chief and the Bear Hunt

Little Chief and Ogopogo

ISBN 978-0-9842291-3-0

To read entry updates about Ogopogo, the famous lake monster in Lake Okanagan, British Columbia, Canada, Google "Ogopogo" or go to http://www.ogopogomonster.com for historic facts, photos and eye-witness accounts. Text: ©Delores Topliff, 2011. Illustrations: ©Jessie Nilo, 2011

Published by TrueNorth Publishing
6901 Ives Ln. N.
Maple Grove, MN 55369
www.truenorthpublishingdt.com

Manufactured by Regent Publishing Services,
Hong Kong

Printed 2011 in China
First Printing

Design and layout: Jessie Nilo

Delores Topliff holds graduate degrees in English (nearly matched by history) and teaches in Twin Cities' colleges. Besides writing, teaching, and speaking, she offers consulting and publishing services. She lives in Minnesota. Visit her online at **www.delorestopliff.com**.

The illustrations in this book were made with acrylics over a textured surface of gessoed canvas paper.
Jessie Nilo holds two degrees in illustration and graphic design from Boise State University. She lives in Boise, Idaho with her husband and three kids.
See more of Jessie's artwork at **www.jessienilo.com**.

Away in the hills of the Okanagan
Lived an Indian tribe in its pointed wigwams,
A tribe that had for its chief a man
Who kept food in the food pots, peace in the clan,
Who saved his tribe from a terrible scare
When he fought a horrible Grizzly Bear,
A great big bear with claws three feet long
That he captured with courage and a bear-hunting song,
But Big Chief knew he had won the fight
Because his Creator helped him do it right,

1

Hold that bear in a daring hug,
Turn him inside out for a comfy rug.
Oh, the village rejoiced, they cheered and danced,
They clapped and shouted, leaped and pranced,
And Big Chief's son learned lots that day,
As he gained wisdom his dad sent his way.

Big Chief ruled well and good years came,
Peace and blessing, good hunting, good game,
Deer in the forests, fish in the streams,
Food in the food pots and food in their dreams.
Little brown babies gurgled, they grew fat and strong,
While their parents sang them heaven's songs,
Taught bold courage, made their elders glad,
As Little Chief grew to be just like his dad.

Then Big Chief knew his time was done
And the one to lead now was his fine son,
So Big Chief lay down for his final sleep
Asked the Lord his soul to keep,
And climbed up heaven's mountain peak,
For he was chief of the proud-hearted, bright-feathered, brave-hunting, good faithful Native People.
Boom boom boom boom
Boom boom boom boom
Boom boom boom boom
Boom boom boom boom

Now Little Chief wore a chief's feathers in his hair,
Saved his people from wolves, cougars and bear.
He found good food, good fish, good game,
Built bigger wigwams, made enemies tame,
Roamed woodland trails and golden hills,
Had small adventures and major thrills,

4

Until one day a few years ago
When he met monster, Ogopogo,
An ancient lake beast that scared moccasins off,
Like cave man drawings on very old rocks,

A watery dragon with head long and thin,
Who swam at top speed using flippers and fins,
With monstrous humps looped high in the air
Swishing down the lake without any care,

5

Two scary eyes above a pointed snout,
When he appeared, the natives gave a shout,

6

Canoes turned over, frightened people jumped out,
Sure he would eat them, they scrambled about,
Lost fish and weapons, paddles and shoes,

Little Chief came when he heard the news.
His people screamed, "Kill him, before he kills us!"
They shivered and trembled, quivered and fussed,

Little Chief said, "Quiet," put his hand to his eyes,
Sat on his haunches and stared in surprise
While the thing slapped its tail like a beaver or whale,
Twirled and dipped like a ship with a sail,

Wiggled and slid in a speedy ride,
Hissed and spit in hideous fits,
Opened jaws wide, hid a canoe inside,
Tore up fish nets, emptied traps,
Ransacked streams, knocked wigwams flat,
Splintered houses, pushed down trees,
Stronger than the stormiest breeze,

8

Showed gleaming rows of pointed teeth,
'Til Villagers cried and wailed with grief,
"This monster eats everything far and near
Big fish and frogs, whole pigs and deer.
He might even climb on shore,
Crawl inside each teepee door
Eat us while we sleep, slobber and chew,
Munch and crunch each wigwam through,
Do the nasty things bad monsters do,
Cause instant floods and tidal waves,
Not stop 'til we're all dead in our graves."

So Little Chief sweated, fretted and groaned
Held his head and sadly moaned,
Prayed, "Lord, help me catch this awful beast,
Capture and toast him for a royal feast
Or make him behave and not scare us at least,
For we are your proud-hearted, fast-running,
bright-feathered, scared but praying Indians."
Boom boom boom boom
Boom boom boom boom
Boom boom boom boom
Boom boom boom boom

Little Chief knew he must conquer this foe
Before Ogo dragged them to his cave below
So Little Chief crouched and waited on shore
Studied and prayed, watched two days more,

Ready to hop like a frog, across lake or bog,
Swish like a fish, as fast as he could wish,
Sneak up on the creature, take it by surprise,
Ponder and learn, watch Ogo's eyes.

He paddled his canoe, though he still had fear,
Stood and balanced, lifted his spear,
Aimed and struck the mighty creature's scales,
But his spear bounced off, the monster lashed its tail,
Swamped Chief's canoe with a furious burst
While the whole tribe watched and feared the worst,
But Chief jumped high and dove down deep,
Paddled and kicked, gave a giant leap,

Crouched on shore all night and all day
Not cold nor hunger could drive him away
'Til he finally saw what few humans see,
Not the bravest hunter or native royalty,
Ogo's wife and babies swam up on a wave,
From way down deep in their watery cave,
She and the babies jiggled and bounced,
Teetered and tottered, wiggled and pounced,
Swam happy and laughing, harmless and free,
Did somersault tricks and raced with glee.
Rocked and wobbled, rode their Daddy's humps,
Sprang and splashed, slid down his bumps,

Ogo lowered his head, lifted babies with his mouth
Taught them water tricks, swam north, swam south
Greeted his wife, fed her yummy fish
Carried offspring to shore, met every wish.
While Little Chief gasped, "How can this be?
This scary monster's as nice as me,
He loves his babies and meets their needs,
Protects them with his frightening deeds.
When his family's threatened, he's fierce and brave,
Shoots up fast from his watery cave.
If I invade, he'll just fight back,
Destroy our village in brutal attack.
I can't give up, I must face this foe,
But I need God's wisdom for the strength to go
Outsmart and conquer, even stay alive,
Face Ogo bravely and save our tribe,
Or he'll gobble me up, swallow me inside,

13

Like Jonah who found no place to hide,
I'm the desperate chief of the proud-hearted, fast-running, bright-feathered, brave and praying Native People."
Boom boom boom boom
Boom boom boom boom
Boom boom boom boom
Boom boom boom boom

When Little Chief went to sleep that night,
God answered his prayers with a dream so bright,
Showed Bible stories he could understand
From the One who formed creatures, and people and land.

First came Noah in the ark afloat
When God called animals to that rescue boat
A big floating thing they'd never seen,
But they followed God's voice and walked right in.

15

Next came Daniel in the lions' den
Showing more courage than the bravest man,
Angels shut lions' mouths, they could only purr,
Wave their tails and comb their fur,
But once Daniel was safe, God released them again
And the hungry lions ate up the men!
Through examples and stories Chief understood
How to face Ogo, though his heart thumped like wood,
He must take charge for all to see
Using God's power and authority.

Like Adam in the Garden when the animals came
When God told Adam to choose their names,
He needed wisdom to make fierce things tame,
Gentle and mild, not injure or maim,

So Little Chief gathered his village to pray,
Said, "Our tribe's future is at stake today,
And I believe God's plan will work,
But please stand with me, don't shiver or shirk."
Then he bowed his head and bravely prayed,
Walking forward, though a little afraid,
While Ogo showed off, boasting and proud,
Diving and frolicking, hissing out loud,

But Little Chief stood and lifted his hand,
Prayed for courage, then gave a command:
"You are Ogopogo, but I am your chief,
Submit and obey, or flee like a thief,
But if you let me protect you, peace will fill your days,
I'll rule fairly with God's wise ways,
For I am chief of the bright-feathered, brave-hunting, wise-hearted, God-loving Native People."
Boom boom boom boom
Boom boom boom boom
Boom boom boom boom
Boom boom boom boom

Ogo sent his family to under-lake caves
And watched Little Chief from dazzling blue waves
Advanced and bullied, threatened and dared,
Spattered and sputtered, menaced and glared,
But Little Chief stood, determined and strong,
And softly sang his victory song,
His villagers came, lifting hands up high
While bright glowing lights lit up the whole sky
Heaven's great power grabbed Ogo tight
Though he struggled and shook with monster might.
Thunderbolts rattled, lightning forked the air,
Ogo rolled his eyes, he shrieked in despair
As his strength and fierceness melted away,
Made him weak and helpless, with nothing to say,

20

But warmth and kindness began to prevail.
Made Ogo friendly and cozy, he wagged his tail
Like a dreadful storm becoming sunny day,
Ogo swam ashore to get acquainted and play,
Placed his fierce head on Little Chief's knee,
Let him climb his back in total safety,
Then swish through the lake without even a bump,
Let Chief slide up and down each hump,
Like a man on a dolphin in a wonderful game
Ogo's mean heart couldn't stay the same.
That frightening beast became peaceful and mild,
Playful and fun, like a happy child,
A watery horse carrying a winning chief,
And the people on shore cheered with relief,
Sang and shouted, whistled and danced,
Clapped hands in rhythm, whooped and pranced

As Ogo swam circles, splashed and leaped,
Called his family from caves down deep,
Frolicked and partied all day and night long
In happy friendship singing joyful songs.

For God gave wisdom, a winning plan,
A special assignment for this faithful clan,
To always guard Ogo and his family line,
Live upright and honest, everything would be fine,

Though the rest of the world might shiver in fear,

Little Chief's tribe would protect, revere,
Not tell the world of their special bond
With Ogo's family in this deep lake pond.
Outsiders feared Ogo was fierce and wild
But with Little Chief's tribe he proved jolly and mild,
Gave children rides, taught them to swim,
Became close friends through thick and thin,
And Little Chief ruled for God each day,
With lasting wisdom kept enemies away,
For he was chief of the brave-hearted, bright-feathered, kind, happy, true-believing Native People.
Boom, boom, boom, boom,
Boom, boom, boom, boom
Boom, boom, boom, boom,
Boom … boom … boom.

24